The Kings of the Backyard

By Kristian William Wright

Contents

Pre-Amble

We are all called to live out the hero's journey. Some of us are called through taking on responsibility, others, through starting a family. Most of us are called on the back end of some tragic event or heartache. It is this journey that enables us to assign greater meaning to our existence than merely the fact we exist.

I wrote most of this screenplay in 2023 at the age of 33 while I was recovering from Thyroid Cancer. I went in for surgery to have my thyroid taken out alongside a significant number of lymph nodes that were all found to be cancerous. My ex-partner, who was 8 months pregnant with our daughter at the time, had to watch me face one of the hardest trials of my life. All of this came almost directly after the death of my father.

This time was extremely difficult for everyone involved and forced me to look at the world through a different lens. As the saying goes: 'A healthy man wants a thousand things, a sick man only wants one.' Little did I know that my cancer battle, the death of my father and all of those struggles were just the beginning of what would become a tragic few years marred by ill-health, loss and destruction.

In my youth I dreamt of achieving so many exceptional feats and becoming someone of great renown. I thought I would start my adult life as a famous musician, travelling the globe, connecting with thousands while conquering the entertainment business. Then, I figured I'd hit middle age and begin my life of service as a politician and then end my life as a great, yet controversial figure who changed the world in his time. Yet these days, after all I've seen and been forced to endure, I find myself longing for a simple life. One that is full of time with my daughter, family and friends.

I am slowly building this life, yet the wounds of these last few years remain. Analogous to Tolkien's Lord of the Rings, the character of Frodo, after he had destroyed the ring and rebuilt his home in the shire ushering an era of peace, was still tormented by the evil he was forced to endure. The Morgul blade that pierced his chest at the start of his journey caused him untold suffering until he chose to sail to the undying lands. It is encounters with true evil that man has always had difficulty reconciling.

Yet despite their impact, struggles and genuine encounters with evil are essential to the hero's journey. It is in these moments that we truly find out who we are. The walls that we built around ourselves to keep the chaos of the world out, get torn down to reveal abundant lands yet to be explored and the promise of meaning deeper than we could've ever conceived of prior.

Although some of these encounters may leave a scar, in my case both metaphorical and physical, provided you pick a path and commit to walking it regardless of its dangers, your tenacity and desire to go on will take you from the helpless child to the conquering hero. From immaturity to maturity.

Unlike Frodo, I am not ready to sail to the undying lands yet.

I hope that this story assists you to realise that you are already on your hero's journey. Your story is valid; you are important and what you do truly matters in this life and the next. I invite you to reflect on some of the horrendous and difficult things you have been forced to endure and to remember that you overcame them, despite the odds being against you and despite having every reason to give up. I hope that through this exercise you realise that surviving those horrors could only be described as heroic.

I hope that this story hits home that meaning can be found in the mundane, particularly if your everyday routines are in service of something greater than yourself.

We may not have it in us to rule nations or play in famous rock bands. We may not ever be awarded medals for deeds of renown or even be remembered after we are gone. Those exceptional things take exceptional people and well, maybe you don't want to be, or you're simply not exceptional. Either way, if you're trying, if you're showing up for your friends and family, if you're taking on responsibility and searching for meaning in your life and you've managed to make it this far. You are a hero to me. I invite you to sit back on your thrown (aka. that old chair you bought on sale from bunnings), fire up the old BBQ, raise your glass and announce a toast to you and yours. Its time for you to take you place amongst the great and renowned Kings of the Backyard.

Now enjoy this stupid shit I wrote while recovering from cancer!

Disclaimer

This script is written as satire.
None of the political views expressed
by the characters in this film are held
by the author.

Opening Scene

We open on a montage of 30 something year olds doing 30 something year old things like working, dropping off kids, driving etc. Sitting at a pub watching footy, having a bbq, falling asleep with babies on them. This is middle class Australia.

Fade In

The Kings of The Backyard over the following scene

Neil sitting on at a train station smoking a cigarette. He is dressed in tradesman/ painters' outfit. A train arrives and goes in front of the camera.

Cut to

Kris having just woken up is in front of a mirror looking at himself. He tenses his titties and then gives one a squeeze and pulls a look of disgust.

Cut to

Jonesy cruising around on a ride on mower drinking a beer.

Cut to

Neil on the train grooving to some tunes on his way to work.

Cut to

Kris in a robe booting his computer up. There is a doctor's letter next to his computer that states his cancer diagnosis. He looks worried/pensive.

Cut to

Jonesy using a whipper snipper. He starts playing air guitar with it.

Cut to

Neil painting a house.

Cut to

Kris is on his computer still in a robe having what appears to be an official work conversation.

Kris: You know what it's like, still jerking from home!

Cut to

Neil in the bottle shop buying a 6 pack and a pack of cigarettes.

Shopkeeper:(thick Australian accent) $230 bucks thanks mate

Neil:(blown away by the cost looking flabbergasted. He also has a thick 'bogan' Australian accent) Are you serious? $230 bucks for 6 cans and a pouch? You've lost ya shit!

Shopkeeper: You want em or not?

Neil: Yeah ring em up (mumbles under his breath). Dickhead.

Shopkeeper: *(clearly heard him but maintains a customer service smile)* Support your own addictions mate.

Neil flips off the Shopkeeper as he leaves the store.

Cut to

Kris Still on the phone 'working'

Kris: I'm just living the dream mate. Trouble is I don't know who's dream it is! When you work it out can you play him some soothing music or something?

Cut to

Neil walking up to an outdoor couch that Kris is already sitting on. He offers Kris a drink that Kris declines and then starts rolling a smoke. Jonesy is cooking up a storm on the bbq.

Scene 1:
Meet the boys

Fade to

Close up of flames on the bbq.

Jonesy is cooking up a storm while Kris and Neil stand on either side of him watching the hotplate intently

Jonesy: (satisfied tone)How good is this looking boys?

Kris and Neil exchange a cheeky look to each other and then start ribbing Jonesy

Neil: I think you need to turn that sausage their mate.

Kris: Yeah, mate it's starting to look a little roasted.

Jonesy: (annoyed) As if you would know.

Neil: It's just that you always burn the bbq Jonesy.

Jonesy: (even more annoyed) Fuck off, I never do!

Kris: Is it me of is it getting a little Smokey in here?

Jonesy:(frustrated grunt)

Kris: Have you seen that hot plate? It's like watching the news on Black Saturday.

Jonesy: (long protracted gasp) that was a national tragedy!

Kris: Too close to home for you mate? LA wildfires then.

Neil: Hahaha I can see Mel Gibsons house burning down next to the steak.

KRISTIAN WILLIAM WRIGHT

Scene 2:
A Path Forward

The boys are sitting around a table with plates full of burnt bbq meat, having a beer, except for Kris who is having a cup of tea.

Neil:(mockingly) oooh having a little tea are we. Ooooh Fancy man.

Kris: (firmly) I will not be judged by you! You charlatan.

Neil: Do you even know what a charlatan is?

Kris pulls a face like he is mocking Neil and makes mocking sounds then Jonesy interrupts as if he is completely fed up.

Jonesy: Is this all our lives are? Shit jokes, Bbq's and beers?

Neil:(excitedly) FUCK YEAH!!

Jonesy: I'm serious boys, we need more. We deserve more.

Kris: (flat and very matter of fact) No one deserves anything Jonesy. It's our lot in life to get up every morning and spread our cheeks for the cock of commerce.

Neil, Jonesy and kris both have a little giggle

Jonesy: (composing himself) Seriously though, we are 35 years old and what has any of us achieved?

The camera pans to look at Kris and Neil looking as if they are truly contemplating what Jonesy is saying until kris responds with……

Kris:(cheekily) Well, you've built the sloppiest rig I've ever seen!

Kris taps Jonesy on the belly

The camera shows Jonesy's face turning red with rage and about to smack Kris then turns to Neil who has detected the animosity in the air and is about to de-escalate the situation.

Neil: Come on Kris, I think he is onto something. I paint houses all day just so I can buy booze, I put on a gallery when I was a kid but that was 15 years ago. Jonesy rides a Jims mower all day, at least that's who he claims Jim is. Could be that he just rides Jim all day.

The camera snaps to kris who spits out a mouthful of tea at this subtle insult on Jonesy

Neil continues: And I haven't seen you wear anything other than shit stained underwear for the last 3 years kris. Seriously mate, working from home has not been kind to you.

The camera snaps back to kris who nods in agreement.

Neil continues: Maybe we should do something that matters. I want to leave a legacy on this world.

Camera returns to kris

Kris: (matter of fact as if this is a normal response) I donated jizz a few times. They got like 50 viable donations a pop. I've got legacies all over the country.

Camera returns to Neil

Neil: (frustrated) Not like that you idiot.

Kris: They call me powerballs down the clinic, like the lottery mate. I hit the jackpot every time. 20 million sperms.

Neil: (scowls at Kris) I mean like a piece of art! Like the Mona Lisa or the Girl with the Pearl Earing.

Kris: (Immediately quips) Oooh, I gave your mum a pearl necklace once!

Camera snaps to kris who is giggling at his own joke like it was actually funny

Neil: (even more frustrated) I can't deal with this idiot.

Kris senses he has pushed Neil to the limit now with stupid retorts and concedes.

Kris: Alright, alright guys, I'm done. What is it exactly that you want to do?

<h1 style="text-align:center">Scene 3:</h1>

<h1 style="text-align:center">Famous animator</h1>

Throughout this scene, Neil describes the type of cartoon he wants to make. As he describes it, the animation unfolds before the audiences eyes.

Neil: (a little tentative) Well, I want to make an animated movie.

Kris: What like toy story?

Neil: Kind of.

Jonesy: (interested) Hmmm you got my attention mate. What would it be about?

Neil: It would be about these three men but they have children's personalities and are the size of children

Jonesy: Wait, are their dicks child sized too?

Kris: (quickly quips) Trust you to think of their dicks uncle creepy.

*As Jonesy says this the **cartoon boys** all of sudden grow huge dicks and the **cartoon boys** wink when kris calls Jonesy uncle creepy*

Neil: They have just average size dicks Jonesy.

*At this comment, the **cartoon boys** dicks disappear, and they look very disappointed.*

Neil: And these boys are going to be like superheroes what like go around fighting burglars and stuff.

*The **cartoon boys** get capes and underwear on the outside like Superman. Then it shows a burglar in a stripy shirt with a mask on.*

Neil: But the burglars aren't humans. They are like fox's dressed in kilts with no undies on underneath so every now and then you can see their ball bags.

*The **cartoon** shows a fox with a burglar mask on a trench coat and two very blue balls hanging out the bottom of the trench coat.*

Kris: (Lets out a bewildered laugh) What?

Neil: Then one of them gets married to like a rich widow who looks like Sophie Monk (or alternative washed up wrinkly celebrity).

the cartoon shows one of the boys getting married to a ball bag in a wedding dress.

Kris: Aw man, I dunno what the fuck you are talking about.

Neil: (continues) Then she takes all their money so the boys have to team up with the ball bag burglars from before to get their cash back. Only the ball bag burglars double cross them and they get robbed again.

cartoon *- The ball bag burglar runs off with a bag on money while the **cartoon boys** look super confused at the camera.*

They continue to stare at the camera as we hear Jonesy say

Jonesy: Are you having a stroke?

At this comment the cartoon fades back to Neil who is staring off into space giggling and repeating ball bag burglars over and over

Kris: (interested) I mean, I like the idea of an animated movie. But I think it's pretty clear that you can't write for shit.

Jonesy: Far too many ball bags.

Neil:(to Kris) Didn't you do like English at uni or some shit?

Kris: Yeah, I'll bang out a script for us, right after I'm done banging ya dad (directed at Neil). Sound good?

Neil: Alright!

Jonesy: What am I gonna do?

Kris: (jokingly) Film me fucking Neils dad so we can finance this thing!

Jonesy looks bewildered as Neil and Kris let out a laugh

Kris: In all seriousness though, you're the only one that's any good with money mate. Neil blows it all on booze and I can't stop buying old nature documentaries on Beta Max.

Jonesy: Seriously? Beta Max? (Jonesy pauses for a second out of bewilderment)

Kris: They look so much better on Beta Max.

Jonesy: I don't really want to do the cash side mate.

Kris: You're the only one who can get us the money Jonesy. It's decided, You're on financials.

Neil: WE MAKING A MOVIE BOYS!!

Scene 4:
Script time

Opens on Kris staring at himself shirtless in the mirror again. He is squeezing one of his titties and making mocking noises while looking at himself in disgust.

Kris: (inner monologue) I can't believe I have tits now. Proper moobs. My 30's are off to a terrible start.

Kris sits back in front of his computer looking really concerned. He is holding the letter confirming the diagnosis of cancer and looking genuinely scared.

Neil busts through the door with a beer in his hand that is sloshing all over the place. He startles Kris who quickly puts the letter under the desk.

Neil: (Loudly and immediately after pretty much kicking the door in) Have you finished my script yet motherfucker?

Kris: (looking shocked and frustrated) It's been one day, did Da Vinci rush the Sistine Chapel? Did Tolkien rush the Lord of the Rings?

(Dramatically) Did Cardi B rush Wet Arse Pussy? I don't think so.

Neil: Alright, alright sorry

Kris: I'm just saying, once in a generation genius only comes along when a truly exceptional person is given the time to develop and mature his ideas like a fine wine.

(Neil looks confused)

Kris: Luckily for you, I'm borderline retarded. Here's your script.

Neil: Aw mad!

Kris starts singing wet arse pussy and dancing in his chair while Neil
grooves around.

Kris: Bring a bucket and a mop for this wet arse pussy!

Neil: So what is it about?

Kris: Well, it's about us. A love letter to your average Australian. An epic story about 3 blokes working out what they're gonna do with their lives now that their 20's are over.

Neil: Ah yeah.

Kris: One has a family; one is hooked on booze and the other just can't work out where he fits in the world and what's missing from his life.

Neil: Nice! Also, fuck you. I know where I fit in the world.

Kris looks at Neil as if he stupid as Neil has been holding a beer the whole time

Kris: But in the end, they discover that its ok to be average and that looking after themselves, each other and their communities is the key to a good life. It's called, 'The Kings of the Backyard.'

The whole time Kris was describing the movie, Neil was opening a pack of ciggies and getting ready to light a smoke while trying not to spill too much beer. As Kris finishes describing the film, Neil throws his cigarette packet rubbish on the floor.

Kris: (Angrily and clearly thinking about his own situation) Ay, quit littering. We gotta save the planet. It's bad enough you are personally responsible for widening the ozone layer with all the chemicals from them cancer sticks. You can give others cancer with em arsehole!

Neil: Your just mad I get more pussy than you.

Kris: Bullshit!

Neil: (lights his smoke) I'm literally fucking mother earth in the ozone hole as we speak!

Neil turns and theatrically walks out of the room while flipping Kris off.

KRISTIAN WILLIAM WRIGHT

Scene 5:

You're always gonna be a piece of shit to me

The scene opens on Jonesy in a nice shirt that's buttons are barely holding on around his midriff. He is having dinner with his parents, and he is about to tentatively break the news that he is going to make a movie with his mates to his dad.

Jonesy: *(looking nervous)* so I was talking to the boys the other day and we came up with an idea to make some serious cash.

Jonesy's Dad (Clint): *(Sarcastically looking over at Jonesy's mum)* Aw this will be good.

Jonesy: Im serious Dad!

Clint: *(speaking to jonesy's mum)* What was it last time Sheila? They thought they could make millions off selling bath water?

Cut to

Jonesy, Kris and Neil in a bath together soaping each other up. This scene looks extremely gay as the boys' giggle and talk.

Jonesy: Wait, this isn't gay right?

Kris: Nah mate, just think of it as a Spa with no bubbles. Now grab that soap and rub me down baby! (Kris winks)

Neil: We are gonna get so rich off this boys!

Cut back to

Jonesy at the table with his dad Clint.

Jonesy: It was an internet sensation dad, I thought we could do it too.

Clint: (continues to berate Jonesy) And then that Kris bloke thought he could sell his cum to a sperm bank. You donate in this country. You don't get paid for donations. That's literally in the definition of a donation!

Jonesy: (jumps to Kris's defence) Give him a break dad. He had a genuine surplus. Not to mention they advertise it as a bank. That's where you get loans and you put your cash and stuff. You can see the thinking behind that can't you?

Clint:(*shaking his head*) Son, your mates are borderline retarded, and you're not far off yourself. I should've known you were special when I caught you trying to stick a toothpick up the cat's arse.

Jonesy: (heightened tone) I was 3 years old!!

Clint: (a little firmer than before) Either way son, you blokes are a few fucks short of an orgy.

Sheila: (promptly shouts) Clinton! Tone it down please.

Clint:(*Winks at Jonesy's mum*) Sorry Sheila.

Jonesy: It's different this time Dad, we have a plan and an idea and everything.

Clint: (*Sighs and lets out a big breath*) Lay it on me.

At this invitation, Jonesy pulls out a pad of poster paper from under the table that has a drawing of the cartoon.

Jonesy: We're going to make a movie dad.

(Clint frowns and looks at Jonesy in disbelief)

Jonesy: It's called 'The Kings of the Backyard.'

(Jonesy turns the page to a picture of the characters doing all kinds of crass, childish things Neil and Kris would find funny like the boys farting, peeing on things and flipping off the camera etc.)

Jonesy: It's about these boys who are adults, but kid sized and they go on adventures.

     KRISTIAN WILLIAM WRIGHT

*Jonesy turns the page and it's a picture of the boys on a pirate ship with one of them
as the captain.*

Jonesy: Essentially. It's a story about guys like us who are doing everything they can
to look after themselves, each other and everyone else pretty much.

Clint: *(looks extremely confused)* But their child sized?

Jonesy: trust me dad, that will appeal to the kids of today for sure.

*Turns the page to one with a graph that has 'the kids' written on the bottom and 'heaps
of dollars' on the other side. The graph starts off at $100 and finishes at 10 million.*

Jonesy: As you can see, we are expecting that the movie will make like an easy 10
million dollars.

(Clint has a look of utter disbelief on his face)

Jonesy: We based that figure on the fact shit like Ms. Marvel made money.

*Jonesy turns the page to one that says at the top 'INVEST WITH US and underneath
it says, 'this is the last day of the rest of your life.' Jonesy is unaware that this
doesn't make sense.*

Jonesy: And all we need to get this project off the ground is a small investment from
you dad. For this investment, we are willing to give you 5% of the film's total revenue.
That's a million dollars! *(unaware that this doesn't add up)*.

*Clint's face softens a little bit. Then he starts to smirk with a really evil grin on the
side of his mouth.*

Clint: (curiously) How much of an investment?

(Jonesy mumbles so that Clint can barely hear him)

Jonesy: Thirtythousanddollars

(Clint Leans over the table and gets closer to Jonesy's face)

Clint: (a little firmer) What was that?

(Jonesy continues to mumble)

Jonesy: Thirtythousanddollars

Clint is now around an inch from Jonesy's face. Clint has started to go red in the face and says angrily

Clint: Spit it out kid, how much?

Jonesy takes a deep breath and clearly states.

Jonesy: Thirty, Thousand, Dollars. Please Daddy.

Clint sits back down slowly while staring Jonesy directly in the eyes. There is an awkward silence as Jonesy looks at his dad trying to work out what he is thinking. Clint remains dead pan but Jonesy's mum who is in the middle of the two looks genuinely scared.

Out of nowhere, Clint starts screaming in rage.

Clint: THIRTY THOUSAND FUCKING DOLLARS? ARE YOU MAD?

Sheila: (pleading) Clinton please

Clint: No, Fuck that, he needs to hear this, Sheila!

Jonesy starts looking very sheepish.

Clint is now standing up out of his chair completely enraged.

Clint: I have one son who is a doctor that hangs out with surgeons and bankers, and then I've got this other one (pointing at Jonesy) who hangs out with a simpleton and a wannabe cum salesman!

When are you going to get your life together? You've got a kid for fuck's sake. I've tried everything with you!!

Jonesy doesn't even consider what Clint just said. He chooses instead to double down on the idea

Jonesy: Dad, I'm telling you, this is the opportunity of a lifetime!

Clint: (escalating) Opportunity of a lifetime? I'll give you the opportunity of a lifetime!!

Jonesy: (with an air of moral superiority) You're not making any sense Daddy.

Clint: (absolutely enraged) I'm going to give you the opportunity to leave my house without me jamming my foot up your arse!

Jonesy stands up from the table and points authoritatively at Clint.

Jonesy: I'm serious Daddy! You better give me that Thirty Thousand Dollars right the fuck now or I'm gonna.

Looks around the table in rushed confusion.

Jonesy: Throw this shitty chicken dinner on the ground.

Jonesy picks up a full leg and partial chicken arse and points it in clints direction. The whole time this is going on, Jonesy's mum looks horrified

Clint: Shitty? How dare you insult your mothers cooking!

There is a pause where Jonesy stares at Clint angrily and Clint stares back the same.

Clint: (low growl) I fucking dare you.

Jonesy throws the chicken leg weakly at the wall like he really didn't want to but had backed himself into a corner. He instantly looks scared and turns to run. Clint chases Jonesy around the table and screams.

Clint: Get the fuck out of my house and never come back!!

End Scene mid-way through clint chasing Jonesy.

<h1 style="text-align:center">Scene 6:
The aftermath</h1>

This scene opens on Neil Ripping a huge cone (bong/water pipe) off a table. Next to the cone is a packet of corn chips and multiple open boxes of condoms. Kris is sitting next to him watching a Beta Max clip of a nature documentary narrated by a David Attenborough type voice on an old CRT TV. David is describing the social structures of chimpanzee troupes. Jonesy walks through the door and looks over Kris's shoulder.

David Attenborough: 'The alpha male proceeds to insert his penis into the anus of the other male chimps in his troupe. This is not an act of homosexuality but rather, a display of dominance.

Kris Looks up at Jonesy and says.

Kris: See Jonesy, it's not gay, it's about dominance.

Kris winks and blows a kiss to Jonesy and chuckles to himself.

Jonesy Shakes his head at Kris and claps his hands to get Neil's attention as Neil is staring off into space stoned.

Jonesy: Now listen up, I'm so sorry boys, I really tried but I couldn't get the money we need to make the movie.

Kris: (nonchalant) Ah yeah, you don't need to worry about that, I forgot to tell you. Neils Nan died last week and left him a metric shit tonne of cash.

Neil is looking extremely pleased with himself.

Niel: (excitedly) We bought some chippies, some condoms, booze, weed and we subscribed to like 50 only fans. So, you could pretty much say we are ready to fuck!

Jonesy: Pfft, watching aint doing. Also, gross.

Kris: Yeah, we got 30k left to make the movie, so you're pretty much fired from your role as producer.

Jonesy:(looking confused) I didn't even know I was the producer. Just thought I was on cash.

Kris: Clearly, we have made the right choice in letting you go.

Jonesy: You mean I didn't have to hit up my psycho dad for money?

Neil: Nah man

Jonesy:(half angry, half sad) He attacked me Neil. He disowned me. I can't ever go back to my childhood home. Ever. Why didn't you tell....

Kris cuts off Jonesy

Kris: HEY! (pauses angrily) At least your Nan didn't die.

Jonesy has a look of realisation. He puts his hand on Neil's shoulder as he says quietly and tentatively.

Jonesy: Oh shit, yeah sorry to hear that Neil, you ok

Neil spins his chair around, jumps up and yells directly in Jonesy's face.

Neil: I'm rich bitch!! Fuck your dad, fuck your family and fuck you!!

Neil flips Jonesy off. Kris is pissing himself laughing as Jonesy makes a fist like he is about to punch Neil in the chin. He takes a breath and calms himself, releasing the fist.

Jonesy: (disappointed and angry) Real nice guys, you know, maybe my dad was right, you guys are holding me back. Especially you Kris.

Kris looks half amused and half upset.

Kris: What? Why me?

Jonesy: You latched on to me when we were young, and I didn't know any better. You constantly hit me up for cash and to help you put your life back together every time you get dumped. I'm sure you've taken years off my life with your bullshit. You're like fucking cancer! Just stuck to me. Draining away my will to live.

Kris: (light heartedly and matter of fact) I don't know about all that man, but I do have cancer.

Jonesy: And what's more, wait... what?

Kris Still light heartedly states very matter of fact.

Kris: Yeah, I got throat cancer man, gotta get it cut out, have some radiotherapy or some shit. Been meaning to tell you guys but I was waiting for the right time.

Jonesy:(flustered) And how is this the right time?

Kris: You said cancer. It made me think of it. By the way, can one of you come with to the surgeons on Monday?

Neil:(Happily states) I'll come with ya cancer boy.

Kris: (upbeat) Cheers man.

Jonesy: (very serious) Fuck, this is serious Kris, you could die.

Neil: The throat goat will never die!

Kris starts laughing.

Jonesy:(Freaking out) Have you told your mum? Seriously man this is fucked up.

Kris: (a little rattled) It's nothing man, stop freaking me out.

Neil: Gonna bulk like hulk on that radiation!

Kris: Fuck yeah!!

Scene 7:
The Surgeons Office

Opens on Neil and Kris sitting in front of a surgeon as he looks at a picture of the cancer in Kris's neck and is explaining what the process is for its treatment.

Surgeon: So essentially, we are going to make an incision from up by your ear down to the bottom of your throat. Then we are going to snip here and cut their until we get all the tumours out.

Kris: (confused) Wait tumours? I thought I only had one.

Surgeon: Well, I can see around 8 on this scan but there's a good chance that there's gonna be a few more stray's that we will find once we get in there.

Kris looks genuinely scared but attempts to use humour to mask his fear.

Kris: Jesus! It's a full-blown cancer party in there. No wonder my throat feels like it's on fire.

Neil starts singing part of Blood Hound Gangs – Fire Water Burn.

Neil: Da roof, Da roof, Da roof is on fire!!

Kris joins in and they sing triumphantly and loudly together.

Kris and Neil: We don't need no water let the mother fucker burn!!!

Kris and Neil chuckle at each other and give each other a high five. The surgeon interrupts them as he is getting frustrated with 35 year olds acting like 15 year olds.

Surgeon: (Firmly) I don't think you really understand the gravity of the situation Mr. Wright. Even after we cut out the tumours, you're probably going to need radiotherapy, maybe even Chemotherapy. The recovery from this is going to be months, if you recover at all.

Kris pauses and looks seriously over at Neil. It is a look of genuine fear. Neil sees this and attempts to break the tension.

Neil: So, the cut your making, will it leave a scar on the front of his neck like he's been in a knife fight?

Surgeon: The scar will be substantial yes.

Neil: Cool!

Kris: That is cool!

Kris and Neil look approvingly at each other.

The Surgeon is shaking his head disapprovingly as he starts looking at his computer to book in the surgery.

Surgeon: I've booked you in for surgery on Friday three weeks from now.

Kris: (quips) Oooh Fridays don't work for me doc. I shave my balls on Fridays.

Kris and Neil giggle.

The *Surgeon is starting to become enraged by this. He throws in mouse on the desk then turns to face Kris directly.*

Surgeon: (sternly) What part of you are dying of cancer don't you understand Mr Wright?

Kris grasps his jaw and pulls a concerned face. He looks even more scared than before. He looks to Neil for re-assurance. Neil meets his gaze and mirrors the fear but then detects that he must diffuse the tension before Kris becomes emotional.

Neil chooses to *butt into the conversation and make a highly inappropriate joke.*

Neil: Can he use his make a wish on hookers?

Kris instantly replies and looks at the surgeon with wide eyed hope. He jumped in on the joke as it made him feel better.

Kris: Oooh, Doc?

Surgeon: Those are for children. You disgust me.

Scene 8:
On with the Show

The scene opens on the boys watching and discussing the show. They are gathered around a shitty old laptop with Neil in the middle drawing up the characters in Microsoft Paint. Jonesy and Kris are on either side of him providing input.

Neil is drawing the character of Kris. He draws him with big titties.

Jonesy: Damn! Look at them titties

Neil: You could just push those things together and just oooh

Neil acts out a bunch of vulgar acts he would perform on Kris's metaphorical cartoon breasts.

Jonesy: (increasing in laughter) Hahaha yeah. Get nasty with them norks Neil.

Neil: Squeeze them baps while I fap.

At this comment both Jonesy and Kris look at Neil perplexed until Kris breaks the tension by saying.

Kris: Not unless you buy me dinner first.

Kris face changes from cheeky to a little annoyed.

Kris: Can you please make them jugs less full and more like those mini milks you get in a hotel?

Jonesy: (High pitched condescending tone) oooh Mini Milks.

Kris: Mmmmmmini Milks! Yummy!!

Neil: No dice! they too nice!

Neil says this as he gives kris a little nipple squeeze in real life.

Kris: piss off mate. Speaking of breast milk, how's your kid going Jonesy?

Jonesy: Not bad

Neil: You should really go home and see it at some point. You've been here for 3 days! The place is starting stink.

Jonesy: I would but me Mrs said I'm more of a hinderance than a help. Apparently, a baby can't be a designated driver.

Cut to

Jonesy sitting on the back of a ride on mower drunk as a skunk while his baby sits up front on his lap 'driving.' They run over a whole manner of back yard objects like frisbees and a cricket bat etc.

Fade back onto kris looking sternly at Jonesy.

Kris: Hey Jonesy (Inquisitively), Have you tried your wife's breast milk?

Jonesy: (pulls a look of disgust) Eeew no way!

Neil: Everyone tries the breast milk Jonesy

Joensy: (Jonesy continues to look disgusted) How would you know?

Neil: I tried my sisters when she popped out her last crotch goblin.

Kris: Straight from the tit I heard.

Jonesy: (Disgusted) That's fucking gross.

Kris: Don't be such a child Jonesy. It's just Incest. But seriously, you've gotta try the breast milk. I'm gonna try it when I'm round your place next.

Jonesy: Like fuck you are!!

(Kris pulls a sucking face and Jonesy)

Kris: Mmmmm yum yum yum yum.

Neil: Don't let him do it Jonesy, your wife will catch breast cancer.

Kris: you can't spread cancer through sucking titties Neil.

Jonesy: (cuts off Kriss) you CAN get it from sucking dick, which is why yours is choking you like 'Big Dick Shannon' would choke ya.

Kris: Who's big dick Shannon?

Jonesy: Shannon Noll mate, rumour has it he cruises the outback tearing fanny. I heard him say you were next in his last interview.

Neil: (sings)What about me?

All the boys have a giggle

Kris shows a little bit of frustration, his brave façade is starting to crack

Kris: We should really look at making some progress on this thing. Might be the last thing I ever make and were running out of time.

Neil: Don't worry David Bowie!

Kris: I don't get it.

Jonesy: (Jonesy in a low serious tone) David Bowie died of cancer.

Kris: (with a grimace) Aw that's Grim!!

Neil: (Happily)I'll finish it later; I got a date!

Cut to

A flashy transition screen comes up that says 'Ooooh A Date!'

Scene 9:
Cheeky little ride

Kris is riding his motorcycle down the road thinking about life now that he is dying of cancer. The below are narrated as Kris's inner monologue over the scene.

Kris: Man, can't believe I've got cancer at 33. I've barely dipped my wick in the great puss of life. Seems I 'm destined to dry hump my way out of existence.

At this point kris pulls up at the lights and looks into the car next to him to see a head moving up and down in the window and the driver pulling looks of pleasure. The driver is getting a BJ in the front seat.

Kris: (getting a bit flustered/excited) Oh man, is that guy getting head? Ha Ha that's crazy! What a legend...

Kris accidentally makes eye contact with the guy getting head.

Kris: (Frantically concerned) Oh fuck I've just made eye contact with him. Fuck what do I do? I'll wink at him to ease the tension. Yeah give him a cheeky wink hey!

Kris winks at him. The guy looks at him confused.

Kris: (embarrassed) Why the fuck did I just wink at that guy.

As Kris thinks this, the guy finishes up and the person giving him head sits back up straight and wipes HIS mouth. They both look at kris as they smile and wave.

Kris pulls a shocked and slightly amused face as he rides off in a hurry

Scene 10:
Neils Date

Open on Neil having a date with really hippie chick who has an 'Just Stop Oil' t-shirt on and fisherman 'hippie' pants. She has messy dishevelled hair, but you can clearly see through all the dirty hippiness that she is beautiful.

Neils Date: (Talking as if giving a speech to parliament) And all our babies are going to choke on the refuse of corroded dinosaurs. In fact, none of us should be having babies at all if we want to save the planet. There are just too many people as it is. To the point some of us colonise other countries. You know you're a coloniser, right?

Neil:(looking nervous but as always trying to defuse tension) you sure? I just thought I was a painter.

Neil's joke didn't land as Neils Date doesn't have much of a sense of humour.

Neils Date: I'm serious, you do understand what I'm talking about yeah?

Neil: (*Clearly has no clue*) Oh for sure. I believe fully in saving the planet and shit.

Neils Date: That's good because a few of us are gonna glue our Vaginas to some paintings in the national gallery to protest oil on Saturday, you should come along!

Neil is pulling all kinds of looks of disbelief as his date talks. He clearly doesn't like her or even understand what she is talking about but shoots his shot anyway

Neil: Oh for sure. You know, I used to eat the glue right out of the pot when I was a kid. My dad says I'm still nothing but a glue eater.

Neil winks at this horrible date who shoots him a little coy smile.

The waiter approaches.

Neil's Date doesn't allow the waiter to say anything

Neils Date: (impatiently) About time Garson.

Waiter looks shocked at this greeting

Neils Date: I'll have the kale salad. Can I confirm that you use organic tomato's and that the dish is gluten free and ethically sourced?

Still looking a little shook up from the greeting. He clearly has no idea if the dish is gluten free or not. He simply shrugs his shoulders and says.

Waiter: Sure

Neil's date gives a conceited look of acknowledgment. Her nose in the air like she is superior to the waiter.

Neil: (stern bogan voice) I'll have the Parma mate. Just chips, no salad.

The waiter nods, turns and leaves abruptly

Neil's date: (looking disgusted, raised voice) Do you know how bad they treat those chickens? They are locked in cages on top of each other. They are fed their own shit and estrogen till their breasts are so big they can't move anymore. I would never put anything that unnatural in my body. You're disgusting.

Neil: (a little frustrated) Ah fucking hell! Is anything ok with you? Chickens are stupid meat footballs made to be eaten yet you seem to think they should live long and fulfilling lives while we get rid of people? (mockingly)Should we give the chickens equal rights and buy them little chicken hammocks as well?

Neil's date goes to open her mouth to retort but Neil silences her by standing up and placing his index finger over her lips. He keeps his finger on her mouth as he says the following.

Neil: (soft, hopeful tone) Honestly, all I wanted out of tonight was to take you back to mine, snort a bunch of coke and then have some outrageous sex. You just seemed like the type from your bio and photos but if you reckon a Parma's bad, cocaine isn't exactly natural, fair trade or ethically sourced.

Neil: (calm and hopeful again) Look, all that aside, I can say honestly that me and me housemate Kris have been really trying not to widen the hole in the ozone layer lately by throwing our rubbish out and stuff.

Neils date: (changes her look from disgusted to flirty) I'm glad to hear that at least you are trying. You seem to really care about Mother Gaia.

Neils date: And I do like doing lines. Maybe I should come over and check out your composting practices?

Scene 11:
Not Enough Cash

This scene opens with Kris and Niel sitting on that heap of shit couch the movie started with them on. Kris and Neil are looking at Neil's phone as Jonesy approached from out of frame. Neil has a picture of the hippie chick on it with her titties out. Kris looks really excited by what he is seeing.

Jonesy: (shocked)Jesus how did you pull her?

Neil: It was easy man. I just told her I was a climate change activist, and I cared about colons and shit for a few hours.

Jonesy: Colons?

Neil: Yeah colons. Like blokes that take other blokes countries.

Jonesy: (Looking flabbergasted) you're a moron

Kris interjects as if he is the worlds foremost expert on human mating behaviour.

Kris: Actually Jonesy, he's a Sneaky Fucker.

Neil: (Grumpily) That's a bit rude mate

Kris: That's literally a scientific term. I heard it on my nature documentaries.

Neil: What?

While Kris explains the phenomena of a sneaky fucker, a cartoon plays of the boys as gorillas acting out what Kris describes.

Kris: A sneaky fucker is weak male who sneaks in and mates with the females behind the dominant males back. Usually while he is off doing masculine things like protecting the troupe from predators. The sneaky fucker, aka you, acts just like the other female Monkeys so they start to think he is safe. He's just one of the girls right? He understands fashion, he listens to out problems and consols us when we bitch about the alpha.

Cut to

Out of the cartoon where Jonesy and Neil are listening intently to Kris rant.

Kris: He pretends to care about the social media activism trend of the day and so on. Then BAM! He pulls out his junk!

Neil: (frustratingly) What's that got to do with me?

Kris: You only managed to pull her by pretending to be a climate change activist. Essentially, she thought you were safe because you are such a little bitch and then you Sneaky Fucked her!

Neil: (sighs in disbelief) You gotta stop watching those animal shows. It's not about dominance, it's just gay and if your gay, that's cool with us.

Jonesy and Neil both nod in Kris's direction as if they definitely know he is gay.

Kris: (Angrily) Oh go glue yourself to a road Climate Bitch. If you can manage to stop eating the glue first.

Neil: Jokes on you cock, that's exactly what I did!

It is pretty clear at this point that tensions are starting to rise between Kris and Neil over the project. Kris's fears about his cancer are starting to manifest as anger towards Neil.

Neil laughs and Jonesy butts in with the reason for his visit.

Jonesy: (authoritatively) Listen up lads, I've been going over the numbers for the movie and 30k isn't going to cut it as a budget.

Kris: Didn't we fire you as producer?

Neil: I re-hired him after we spent five grand on a replica Back to the Future hoverboard cause you said it's the only this project was ever going to get off the ground.

   KRISTIAN WILLIAM WRIGHT

laughs softly then looks flabbergasted at Neils stupidity. He then shakes his
head in disbelief.

Kris: hahaha yeah.

Jonesy: We are going to need to get more money. I reckon at least another 30k.

Kris: Oh shit.

Jonesy: Now I've been looking into it and Screen Australia do grants for independent movie projects. I've got us a meeting with their primary delegates.

Neil: Hell yeah!

Jonesy: Now this is our only hope, so we need to make sure we charm them.

Neil: Don't worry Jonesy, I'll have them eating out of my arse in no time.

Jonesy: You can't sneaky fuck these folks mate. You better let Kris do the talking.

Neil: (Sarcastically) Yeah that makes sense, let the guy with throat cancer use his voice.

Kris: (shoots Neil an angry look) Lay off the cancer shit will you. Don't worry Jonesy I got this.

Scene 12:
Trying to make friends.

Kris and Neil are

walking along St. Kilda beach on their way to the meeting with the Screen Australia people. They are discussing intently how they are going to manage the meeting when they come across two black guys on towels. Neil just has to make a comment.

Kris: (seriously and sounding stressed) When we get there, like Jonesy said, just let me do the talking ok?

Neil ignores Kris and stops walking as he looks over at two black guy sitting on towels on the sand.

Kris continues to walk and stops abruptly to look back.

Neil starts addressing them.

Neil: (friendly and upbeat) Hey! Nice colour boys! I'm working on my tan this season as well. Going for a nice Grecian bronze.

Black guy: (angrily) What did you just say?

Neil: (still bubbly and friendly) I just wanted to compliment your tan my man. You've achieved the pinnacle of colouration. You've sailed past Naughty Nutmeg to a nice Masculine Mahogany.

Black Guy: (even angrier) Are you fucking serious white fella? Making comments about my colour?

Neil: (*Genuinely confused about how his comments could be considered inappropriate. Almost aggressively*) What? It was a compliment.

Kris: (whispers to Neil) Shut up man.

Black Guy: (angrily) you better get the fuck out of here!

Neil: (trying to calm the situation) Whoa, chill out bro. I didn't mean anything by it sorry.

The guys start to drop their arms and take a less aggressive stance until Neil tries very innapropriately to connect using what he perceives as the correct language.

Neil: Us mob are just like you mob.

Black Guy: You're fucked!

The black guys start chasing Neil and Kris who sprint to the screen Australia office. They run inside and lock the door behind them.

Scene 13:
Woke Miss steps.

The boys sit at a table across from two caricatures of identity politics circa 2023. They/thems who oversee handing out artist grants. One has multi-coloured hair and is rotund. The other is also rotund, covered in piercings with a political t-shirt on.

The boys walk in and sit down.

Chinthia: (rudely) No need to get too comfortable boys, this won't take long.

Rollz:(condescendingly) We here at Screen Australia feel that we have a responsibility to tell only stories of value. We work tireless to raise the voices of minorities and protected classes.

Rollz: I haven't read your script but from looking at you two, I can assume it won't meet our criteria.

There is an extended silence where Kris and Neil look at Rollz and Chinthia nervous and confused. Neil whacks Kris on the side of leg.

Neil: (whispers)Say something.

Kris:(Also whispers) like what?

Niel: Pay em a compliment or something.

Rollz: (interrupts) We can hear you.

At this, Kris pushes his seat back, stands up and clears his throat as if he is about to deliver a presentation that will change their minds.

Kris: (formally) I'm sorry ladies, it seems we have gotten off on the wrong foot.

Chinthia: (angrily and slowly) I am not a lady.

Kris: (again overly formal) My sincerest apologies to whatever you are.

Kris grabs Chinthia's pudgy fingered hand and hold it daintily as he looks it in the eye.

Kris: You are an absolute marvel though.

Chinthia blushes

Neil: (interjects to try and break the tension) Yeah you have the figure of Lizzo!

Chinthia looks initially angry and is about the comment but then she must subscribe to the delusion that Lizzo is beautiful and lets out a slight disgruntled.

Chinthia: *Thanks.*

Kris: (still weirdly formal) And you my dear bear a striking resemblance to Caitlyn Jenner.

Rollz again looks initially angry but must remember the importance of complimenting minority figures.

Rollz: Thanks.

Kris: (Attempts a heartfelt plea after dropping the overly formal tone) look, I appreciate you meeting with us today. I'm sorry that you didn't like our movie. We didn't know that the narrative had to be written in a specific way for it to be made into a movie. We were just trying to make something that we thought was funny and to tell our personal stories because in our heads, everyone's story is important and deserves to be told. Even three fuck ups like us.

At this plea, Rollz and Chinthia appear to soften a little in their approach.

Rollz: Look, you boys seem nice. Maybe you aren't the red pilled incels we thought you were. We can help you workshop your story to make it acceptable for the Australian public.

Neil and Kris both look at each other and let out a mini celebration.

Rollz: (continues) It must raise up the voices of minorities, affirm the power of woman and represent the classes of our nation who have been victims of oppression for far too long including, but not limited to: woman, LGBTQISA+, indigenous and other peoples of colour.

Neil (*Tugs on kris's pants. Kris bends down and Neil whispers in his ear*) I have no idea what the fuck these bitches are talking about.

Kris: shhh We can google it later.

Chinthia: (interjects with the same authority Rollz had) The best way to get your screenplay up to scratch would be to include at least one gay or queer coming out story, one strong female lead and at least one third of your characters must be from a minority or indigenous group.

Kris and Neil both consider this for a second or two. Kris looks as if he is really thinking hard about it.

Kris: Hmmm ok, and how many of those are in our story?

Chinthia: None Mr. Wright.

Neil: (Excitedly interjects) Fair enough. It doesn't sound too hard to fix though! Is a minority like a black person?

Rollz: Not just black people, Asians, Indians and many others.

Kris: She just means people who aren't white Neil.

Neil: So black people work then. Awesome!

Chinthia: (sarcastically) Do you even know any black people?

Neil: We have two black mates, they're literally right outside.

Kris: I don't think that's right Neil, they didn't seem to like us very much.

Rollz: I'm not surprised.

Neil: ooh your character can be questioning if you are gay the whole time. Just like real life.

Neil laughs and points at Kris.

     KRISTIAN WILLIAM WRIGHT

Kris responds annoyed for second but then immediately thinks of a comeback.

Kris: Fuck up idiot! I suppose we could swap your characters gender, and SHE can save the day!!

Neil: (excitedly) and we could make Jonesy's character black. Done!

Rollz: You can't just make a white character black and expect that to be ok.

Kris: (matter of fact) Why not? Disney did it.

At this comment, the Screen Australia staff look absolutely disgusted at the boys.

Rollz: (enraged) Get out of our office right now you homophobic, racist bigots.

Kris: Whoa! Chill, It's just an observation.

Chinthia: I knew under those façades of tolerance that you were just another pair of disgusting straight white men. Your story is not of any value to anyone. Get out now!

Scene 14:
Jonesy's place

Kris, Jonesy, Jonesy's wife Annabelle and Neil are in Jonesy's living room with Jonesy's kid. They are catching up after the disastrous meeting with Screen Australia.

Neil: (*talking about the baby*) She's beautiful mate. It's a beautiful thing being a father.

Jonesy: Thanks mate, by the way boys, I tried the breast milk the other day. It was weird, like sweet and watery.

At this, both Neil and Kris look at Jonesy disgusted. There is a slight pause when Kris says loudly

Kris: YUCK, your disgusting Jonesy.

Neil: (acting like he is grossed out) I can't believe you did that man. What the fuck is wrong with you?

Jonesy: (Looking grumpy and confused and yelling) YOU BLOKES TOLD ME TOO! YOU SAID EVERYONE DOES IT!

Kris: (acting shocked) And you believed us?

Neil: (acting disgusted) I can't work with you anymore Jonesy. You are seriously rank.

Kris: Yeah your fired as producer again.

Jonesy: (starts to catch onto the joke) You guys are full of shit. I'm sick of yas anyway.

The boys all have a bit of a laugh

Jonesy:(*To his wife*) baby, do you mind cutting up some onions for the bbq? I'm gonna start cooking.

Kris: Ash Wednesday inbound.

Jonesy: (genuinely annoyed) Again, with the national tragedies!! Show some respect!

Kris looks over to Jonesy's wife Annabelle with a cheeky look on his face.

Kris: (to Annabelle) You'll have to send what's left of them onions back to England after he's done with them. England won the ashes this year.

Jonesy throws his hands up in the air and storms outside as Annabelle and Kris both laugh at how annoyed he is.

Neil follows Jonesy out to make sure he is ok leaving just Kris and Annabelle in the room.

Annabelle: (To Kris) Here hold the baby for a second.

Kris: (grossed out) Ew I'm not touching that thing. It used to be Jonesy's cum.

Annabelle: (dismissive) Don't be ridiculous.

Kris: (argumentatively) I'm ridiculous? I know what you did to make that thing!

Jonesy's wife hands kris the baby and walks out of the room.

Kris holds the baby under the arms out in front of him awkwardly

Kris: (genuinely worried) Don't you shit on me.

Kris stares awkwardly at the baby who is incredibly cute. Kris starts to talk to the baby

Kris: What are you looking at? You're a funny looking thing ay? I guess your cute though. Which is surprising considering what ya dad looks like. His head looks like a half-chewed foreskin.

Kris gets a cheeky grin on his face

Kris: (cheekily)You're parents are absolute freaks kid. On the night you were conceived, it probably started with pegging, then moved onto some arse eating followed by kissing (kris pulls a face of disgust) and then ya dad would've jumped behind ya mum and busted full doggy style. AAAWHOOOO (Howel)

Baby: *At this the baby lets out a laugh.*

Kris: Yeah that's funny ay? Like a Pug and an English Bulldog. No balls left unchewed.

Baby: *Starts to cry*

Kris: hey hey hey shh shh its ok.

Kris managers to settle the baby in a cute heartwarming moment.

Kris: (softly) See mate, life's not so bad. One day you'll grow up and get a good job, meet a good man like your dad (kris starts to choke up), fuck maybe even do some good in the world. You have to promise me you'll do some good in the world. Not like your uncle Kris. I'm fucking dying kid.

This is the first time Kris said out loud that he is dying. At the admission he begins to show both fear and sadness. He cries hard than before and says the below through choked back tears.

Kris: I never had a family like your dad or made amazing art like your uncle Neil. I never achieved anything. I've got a week left before it could all be over. I'll never have a baby like you. You beautiful amazing creature.

Kris finally and fully breaks down and holds the baby close as he cries. The Baby remains soothed and calm in his embrace as if it knows that he is in pain.

At this point, Jonesy and Neil come back into the room. Kris quickly wipes his eyes on his shoulder and pretends he is fine. Jonesy sees this but knows some things are better left unspoken between men.

Jonesy: She alright mate?

Kris: (trying to hide he has been crying) Yeah we have an understanding.

Jonesy looks at kris concerned but chooses to drop the matter.

Kris puts the baby into her nearby baby rocker now that she is calm.

Jonesy: (hopefully) So, tell me what happened boys. Did we get the cash?

Kris: Well, they didn't like it.

Neil: (disappointedly) They told us our story isn't of any value to the Australian public and called Kris a bigot.

Kris: They called us all kinds of things. Apparently, our stories not valid because it's about average straight white guys or some shit. It's a bit of blur.

Neil: (completely defeated) I've never been more disappointed in my life.

The boys all look disappointed and have moment of silence as Jonesy's wife enters the room and stands between them. She is wearing a t-shirt that says: 'BELIEVE IN YO'SELF GURL'

Kris spots this and his face turns from disappointed to hopeful as Annabelle stands in between him and Neil. Kris jumps out of his seat and points at Anna's titty

Kris: This, this right here Neil. You just gotta Believe in yourself. We can do it!

Neil: We can't man, it's over.

(Kris puts his hand under Anna's titties and holds them up)

Kris: (with urgency) seriously man read it.

Neil: (Stands up out of his chair) fine.

Neil proceeds to lift up Anna's left tit so he can get a closer look for some reason.

Kris: (Grabs Anna's right tit and says excitedly) Do you feel it man?

Jonesy doesn't speak but clearly looks angry/annoyed with his hands out. Its clear he isn't happy with his friends frantically fondling his wife's breasts.

Neil: (now lifting up and dropping Anna's tit) I feel it man, we can do this.

Annabelle smacks the boys over the back of the head and walks away

Both boys rub the back of their heads as she leaves. Neil flops back into his chair still defeated, angry and disappointed.

Neil: I just don't understand why you couldn't have tried harder in that meeting. In fact, you've been checked out this whole-time, it's like you don't care about me or my dreams.

Kris: (Annoyed) Excuse me, but I've been a bit pre-occupied mate.

Neil: (mockingly) drrrrrr cancer blah blah blah. It's all you talk about. You look fine to me.

Kris: (escalating) Are you serious? I'm having surgery in a few days. I could die from this shit and the only thing I'm leaving behind is this movie. I genuinely tried man.

Neil: Well, you blew it. You have never cared about me. You've treated me like a sidekick my whole life.

Jonsey: (calmly) Whoa, take it down boys, I know we're hurting but you don't mean that.

Neil: I've never meant anything more in my life. I'd be better off without you Kris.

Kris: (disappointed and sad) Well you might be about to get your wish. *(Starts tearing up again)* Good luck with your movie.

Kris turns away from Neil and heads for the door. Jonesy calls out to try and stop him.

Jonesy: Kris stop, he didn't mean it.

Scene 15:
Another ride/Surgery prep montage

Kris takes his motorcycle out for a final ride before surgery. He pulls up next to the car that had the blokes who were blowing each other in it from the earlier scene. They both wink and smile at him. He rolls his eyes, lets out a little smile, waves, then rides off.

Fade to

Kris parks his bike in the garage. He hides the key under his toolbox and puts his helmet inside it.

Cut to

Neil erasing Kris's character from the cartoon and looking really concerned.

Fade to

Montage of Kris tidying up the area's from earlier (outside couch/bbq etc.) and getting them in order.

Cut to

Jonesy holding his daughter looking concerned/upset.

Cut to

Neil drinking, smoking and laughing at pictures of him, Kris and Jonesy.

Cut to

*Kris sitting down and writing his bank passwords, laptop passwords etc. He writes
a note to the boys and reads it out aloud.*

Kris: *'To Jonesy, Neil and our fuck head landlord who will likely find this first. On
this day I bequeath to you the only gift I have left to give, the gift of my absence. I
have no money in my bank account and nothing in this house is worth anything.
Fuck you and eat shit. Love Kristian.'*

*Kris smiles and giggles then looks really concerned and scared like he is
about to cry*

*The camera crossfades from his face in this state to his concerned face on the
operating table getting prepped for surgery*

Scene 16:

Surgery

This scene opens on Kris lying on the operating table as a team of people prep him for surgery. He looks extremely concerned as the team around him attempt to calm him.

Surgeon: Mr Wright, can you tell me what surgery you are having today?

Kris: (Nervously trying to diffuse the tension) A sex change.

Surgeon: Really? Don't you already have a fanny?

The Surgeon flicks the tip of Kris's penis over his hospital gown comically.

The Nurses all giggle.

Kris: (lets out a nervous laugh) Sorry doc, I'm just shitting myself. I'm having Tumours cut out from my throat. At least 8 of them apparently.

The nurses fall silent as Kris's words hang heavy in the air.

Surgeon: (*Solemnly*) That's correct Mr. Wright. Now I promise you, that I will do everything in my power to get you through this, but I must advise that there is a chance that you could die.

Kris: I know, thanks Doc.

Surgeon: I'll leave you with Brad your anaesthesiologist and I'll see you on the other side.

Brad comes into kris's view wearing a surgeon's mask and looking down at him.

Brad: (*Very flirty gay voice*) Well hello handsome, nice to finally see you up close.

Kris: (Looks confused) I'm sorry?

Brad pulls his mask down and winks at Kris. Kris realises that Brad is the guy from the car that he sore getting head from his boyfriend and who he waved to again just the day before. Kris has a look of shock and embarrassment.

Kris: oh…ah..hey

Brad: Count to ten honey, you won't feel a thing.

As kris loses consciousness from the anaesthetic he says

Kris: oh shit, doc, protect my anus!

Scene 17:
After Surgery

Kris wakes up in a hospital room with Jonesy standing over him. It's the day after the surgery and Kris is in a lot of pain and not doing well. He has had multiple tumours removed. He has multiple vacuum drains hanging out of his neck, a catheter and a fairly gruesome bandage across his neck.

Jonesy: (softly and nervously) Hey, hey mate. How are you doing? You holding up ok?

Kris: (false optimism) yeah bloke. I feel great. Pretty much healed.

Jonesy: It's alright if you're not, you're in the fight of your life. It's ok to have feelings at this point.

As Jonesy says this, kris breaks down and can no longer hold it together.

Kris: (*breaking down*) This is awful. I'm in hell. Theirs drains coming out of my neck, blood pissing of them, I cant talk properly and theirs a tube up my dickhole for fucks sake. Apparently one of my kidneys is fucked now too. Why me? What did I do?

Jonesy: (solemnly in a soft whispered tone) Nothing man, it was just your turn to suffer. We all have to at some point. Doesn't matter how we've lived or how much good we've done. It's just the nature of things.

Kris: (choking back tears) I know, I just feel like I can't handle it anymore.

Jonesy: (a bit sterner) Well, you need to become someone that can. It's the tough times that make us tougher. Besides, you're on the mend now mate! You got through the surgery! Its going to be ok.

Jonesy pauses and looks at Kris whose tone turns dark, frantic and aggressive.

Kris: No it won't! Don't lie to me. It's only a matter of time until I get sick again or another horrible, life destroying thing happens to me.

Jonesy looks shocked at the negativity coming out of Kris's mouth as he sits back up in his seat.

Kris escalates in intensity and begins to shed some tears of hurt and anguish.

Kris: I just want to die. I pray to my father to take me home. I just want to go home. Let me die please. It would be a mercy at this point. I've done nothing, I have nothing, and everyone would be alright if I went. I'm so lost and weak. I was supposed to die from cancer. I don't know why I let them save me. Let me go. Please. I just want to go home.

Jonesy: (sternly) No.

Kris: Life is nothing but suffering to me now.

At this comment Jonesy stands up out of his chair and begins to well up. His tone is firm yet fragile as he fights back tears to say

Jonesy: Then suffer well. Bare it and when you can't any longer put it on our shoulders. I'm here. I'm in this with you.

Kris: (full breakdown, tears and all) I can't. I just can't anymore.

Jonesy: (puts his hand on Kris's shoulder and makes stern eye contact with him) You gotta dig deep and pull through. It's your responsibility to get better for all of us. You're a man. Men suffer. Stop acting like a child and asking to go home. I can help you, but no one can take this away.

Jonesy looks sternly at Kris as the words hang in the air. Kris starts to pull himself together.

Jonesy: (no longer sad but resolute) So what is it going to be? Are you going to stay the scared, helpless child you were when this all happened to you? Or are you going to be a man and walk out of this hospital with your head held high? A man that survived cancer and came back stronger than ever! That's what I want for you. Don't you want that to?

Kris: (Starts pulling it together) I'm sorry. You're right. I got this.

Jonesy flops back down in his seat exhausted. This is the most emotion either of the boys have ever shown. They are both exhausted.

Jonesy: (nods) Good.

The two sit quietly for a second. Not making eye contact but just being in each other's company Jonesy passes Kris a tissue. The silence is broken when Jonesy says.

Jonesy: Neils outside.

Kris: ah yeah.

Jonesy: He might not say it, but he regrets how everything went down last you spoke.

Kris: (wiping his eyes with a tissue) I'm good man, bring him in.

Jonesy: (yells)OI NEIL!

Neil opens the door and peaks his head in. He has a bouquet of flowers in his hand. He smiles nervously but it's clear that he shocked by what he sees.

Neil: (speaking as if he is directing his communication to an infant) hey buddy, how are doing?

Kris: (short and sharp) I'm alright mate.

Neil: Really? Cause you look like shit.

Jonesy: NEIL! You're not helping

Neil: *(notices the catheter bag)* Is that a bag of your piss? Eew that's fucked.

Kris: (claps back) Drink it bitch.... Hang on, did you buy me flowers?

Neil: Ah.... No

Jonesy: What are these then?

Jonesy points to the flowers in Neils hand.

Neil quickly puts the flowers behind his back.

Kris: *(jokingly)* I can't believe you bought me flowers. Did you get me chocolates too? Did you write me a little card?

Neil: Shut up man, I didn't know what to get ya. Never had a mate almost die before.

Jonesy quickly snatches the card out of the bouquet of flowers.

Jonesy: He did get you a little card kris. Aaw little card.

Kris: Naw it's a gay little card! What's it say Jonesy?

Jonesy: It says 'Sorry mate, I never want us to be apart again. From Neil'

Kris: Why didn't you write 'Love Niel?' Don't you love me?

Neil: shut up

Kris: hahaha we're good man. I'm sorry I got so sensitive. Things got so tough there for a minute that I lost who I was. I still feel out of place, but I'll work it out.

Neil who missed Kris's breakdown looks very confused about it all. Jonesy is watching Kris intensely as he speaks.

Kris: It was all well and good when we were just taking the piss out of each other round the BBQ at home. Fuck I miss that BBQ. And my couch! I just want my regular life back and some good times with the boys!

Jonesy: (wisely) Those times are going to look a little different now mate. You aren't the same person anymore but that's ok. We're meant to change. Tests like the one you're going through, me and me daughter, Neil and the booze, it's like were meant to die and be reborn over and over.

Neil: (Excitedly) Speaking of which, I decided to kick the booze in your honour.

Kris: Seriously? I never thought you'd ever admit to having an issue with it

Jonesy: IIe has mate, so have I. This time I reckon it's going to stick. None of us want to be where you are.

Kris was looking happy but then changed to a sad and downtrodden expression. He thinks for a second then a small smile returns to his lips.

Kris: Well, I'm glad at least one positive can come from this. Congratulations boys, you should be proud of yourselves.

The boys stand on each side of the hospital bed and they all hug it out. Neil sits down next to Kris as Kris passes him his piss bag.

Kris: Hey, hold this will you?

Neil: Eeeew Fuck!

Neil stands up and drops the bag on the ground which is still attached to Kris's penis. Kris gets lurched forward and screams in pain as the bag falls to the floor onto something sharp and bursts open with his urine violently splashing out all over the boys' feet as Neil jumps up on his seat and Jonesy slips in it.

Scene 18:
Outside the hospital

Having drenched Kris's hospital room in urine, the boys have moved to a hospital courtyard. Jonesy and Neil aren't wearing any shoes or pants, just boxer shorts. Kris is in a wheelchair with his hospital gown open and an ice pack on his penis. Neil is having a cigarette as the boys continue to talk.

Kris: So, where's the movie at boys? Can we make it work with the cash we have?

Jonesy: Well, after you went into hospital I went back to Screen Australia and apologised profusely for your actions. They were pretty mad. It's like you insulted their religion or something.

Kris: (Matter of Fact) That's exactly what I did.

Jonesy: Right, well anyway, we were able to work with them to come up with a story that meets their criteria.

Neil: (Satisfied) We finished the movie mate.

Kris: Oh really? That's awesome!

Jonesy: Now it's not exactly how you wrote it, but I think you'll be impressed. We have booked out the local theatre for the premier in a few weeks so get yourself right because we're the guests of honour.

Neil: (excitedly) This is the start of something big boys! We're gonna be famous!

Kris: I'm proud of you guys. I can't wait to see it!

Scene 19:

The premier.

*The scene opens on Jonesy, Kris and Neil giving an interview for a local TV station
out the front of a packed theatre. Chinthia and Rollz are standing next to the boys
as they speak overseeing the interview.*

Reporter: Tonight is the premier of the latest offering from Screen Australia's diverse and inclusive grants program. An animated epic that raises up the voices of the oppressed and victimised groups of our country titled 'The Kings of the Backyard.'

With me here are the creative team behind the film. How does it feel to have made something as important to the culture as I've heard this movie is going to be?

Neil: (matter of fact) Good.

Jonesy butts in.

Jonesy: Well, we thought it was important to spread only the messages that Screen Australia told us too.

Reporter: And Kris, as the writer of the film, can you confirm that the film raises awareness of the struggles that minorities and the oppressed go through?

Kris: I dunno about any that. I just wanted to make a movie.

Chinthia and the reporter start to look concerned.

Kris: (very matter of fact. No aggression in his voice) And honestly, I don't even think you care, let alone know what you're talking about.

*Kris smirked as the reporter glared and began to take the microphone back. Kris
quickly grabbed the microphone to say*

Kris: (conciliatory tone) Look, it's gone through a few rewrites under the instruction of Screen Australia. I haven't seen it so it might. Who knows? Do you know?

Kris points at the reporter and looks at him as if he genuinely thinks the reporter may know.

Reporter: errr um

Chinthia grabs the microphone as the reporter stumbles having just been told the writer of the film hasn't seen it, chose to insult him and to speak in round abouts. Chinthia butts in to save the day

Chinthia: We at Screen Australia work tirelessly to ensure that only valid stories get turned into movies. We assure you that this film will represent the oppressed, minorities and protected classes of our society. Please come on in, the films about to start.

Chinthia hastily rushes the boys away from the cameras.

Cut To

The boys, Chinthia and Rollz sitting in a packed theatre with yummy treats as the lights go down and the film starts. The camera zooms in on the film that starts with a screen that says 'The Kings of the Backyard.' The title has a rainbow over the top of it.

The films audience politely clap.

The first scene of the animated movie opens on Jonesy's character who is clearly white. The screen glitches and Jonesy's character turns black. No other changes to the characters size or look. He just turns from white to black. Jonesy's cooking up a bbq when Kris's character walks in.

Kris's character: Hi I'm Kris and I think I might be gay.

Jonesy's character: (happily) Hi Kris, I support your gayness. I understand your struggle because....

Jonesy's onscreen character pauses and looks down in a really sad manner and says solemnly

Jonesy's character: I am oppressed by the white man.

The camera cuts to Neil in real life. He is absolutely pissing his pants (aka laughing hysterically). Kris is sitting there with his mouth wide open with a look of utter delight across his face and Jonesy is looking at Chinthia and Rollz for their reaction with a cheeky glint in his eye.

Back to the screen. Neils character walks in and he has a beard and is in a dress with high heels.

Neil's character Newlette: I am a strong independent woman, and I don't need no man.

Jonesy's character: I affirm your identity.

Kris's character: you are both stunning and brave.

Cut back to the boys increasingly pissing themselves laughing. Full on knee slapping at this point.

(Cross Fade to show time passing). The boys grinning and holding back laughs and looking at Chinthia and Rollz who look absolutely mortified. On the screen is Newlette giving a speech at a rally full of the usual suspects. People wearing random political cause t-shirts with mutli-coloured hair etc.

Newlette: It seems the cis white men have fucked up the election. I will save the day without the help of any of you stupid men.

The onscreen crowd cheers as Newlette smiles and throws her fist up in the air. The camera cuts to Kris's character and Jonesy's character who are standing in the onscreen audience.

Kris's character: I'm still not sure but I think I might be gay.

Jonesy Character Very good Newlette. The white man are colonizers, they are evil and deserve to be held accountable for what their ancestors did.

Cut back to

The movie theatre where Neil, Kris and Jonesy as they all look at Chinthia and Rollz for their reactions. Rollz is starting to lose their composure.

Rollz: (Freaking out) Can we get this shut off please?

Chinthia: (whispers to Rollz) The crowd will think we made a mistake. Best we just let it play out.

Cut to

Rollz and Chinthia with their head in the hands and the boys still pissing themselves and shaking each others hands etc. All round celebrating.

Cut back to

The movie.

Newlette is standing with a huge gold medal around her neck, holding a key to the city with a badge that says 'Prime Minister' next to Jonesy's character and Kris's character.

Newlette: I told you I didn't need no man. I smashed the patriarchy and saved the election. Now only woman can be in power. There will be no more mis or disinformation on the TV and you won't be allowed to use the internet without giving your biometric data to the government. You are safe now and you will see only messages I approve.

Jonesy's character: (says happily) Down with the colonizers.

Kris's character: (happily) It turns out I am super gay, and everyone is cool with it.

Newlette and Jonesy's characer: You are so brave. We affirm your identity.

A title screen comes up and says 'The End.' It has a ring of people holding hands of all colours and sexual orientations with a rainbow in the middle.

Cut back to the boys literally rolling on the ground laughing hysterically and pointing at Rollz and Chinthia who at this point are practically turning red with embarrassment and rage.

The Audience is clapping politely in the background but theirs not exactly a standing ovation.

The boys get up and start talking with Rollz and Chinthia.

Kris: (sarcastically) So, what do you reckon? Money well spent.

Rollz: (defeated and sad) That was highly offensive, and you know it.

Jonesy: (Sarcastically) It had a strong female lead, a gay coming out story and a minority story. Literally all the protected classes and minorities in one movie. Everything you asked for. You can't say it wasn't a valid story.

Chinthia: (angrily) I am disgusted with what I have just seen.

Kris: Well, you should've let us tell our story. I survived cancer, I literally just nearly died. Neil seems to have kicked a booze habit while I was in hospital and has developed this amazing talent for animation. I mean that was a masterpiece!

Kris lets out a sarcastic laugh. Jonesy and Neil both react in much the same way.

Kris: Jonesy is a family man who worked his youth away just so he could buy his family a home. He turns up for his daughter and his amazing wife. He once drank her breast milk. Super fucking weird and irrelevant but it happened.

Everyone looks at each other confused as to why Kris bought this up.

Kris: See we are just three average guys, doing everything we can to look after ourselves and each other. We aren't perfect, we're stupid, ignorant and we fail a lot. A lot more than most I'd say, but we love deeply and we are trying our best to be better people every day.

The remaining crowd in the cinema at this point are watching and listening intently to this monologue that Kris is delivering.

Kris: We may not have any special titles or belong to any so called 'oppressed' or 'protected' groups, but we are, like most people, regardless of race or sexual identity, trying to get by and to do a little good while we're at it.

Someone in the crowd exclaims.

Crowd Member: Fuck yeah!

Kris nods over in that guy's direction as he realises the crowd is listening.

Kris: (pronouncing louder and more intensely) You may say we aren't special, but I say that we, like everyone in here are worthy Kings of the Backyard!

Kris throws both of his hands in the air and presents them to the crowd.

Jonesy, Neil and Kris along with the entire crowd cheer and celebrate. Popcorn is thrown, people hug and fist pump in the air in victory. This goes on for 10-15 seconds or so.

Kris then with his outstretched arms, signals the crowd to quiet down.

Kris: (intensely towards Chinthia and Rollz) How can you say that our stories have no value?

Chinthia: *(matter of fact like its obvious)* Because your privileged cis white men.

The crowd let out a few jeers and boos.

Kris again signals them to silence. Then points directly at Chinthia's face.

Kris: (sternly) Fuck you racist. Neil, put this heap of shit on YouTube and make sure the public knows Screen Australia paid for it with their tax Dollars.

Neil in his trademark fashion flips off both Chinthia and Rollz. The crowd is again raucously celebrating.

Neil: Yeah fuck you!!

Cut to

The boys walking away in slow motion to rock music with their arms around eachothers backs victorious. Chinthia and Rollz are behind them in background standing their stunned as the crows continues to celebrate.

Cut to

The boys having a cup of tea, toasting with their custom mugs (Neils has a VB logo on it so he can still feel like he is having a beer) and celebrating their victory further.

Cross fade out to the next scene.

KRISTIAN WILLIAM WRIGHT

Scene 20:
The aftermath

This scene opens up on the boys back on the same old couch in the same old backyard that this story started in. Jonesy's kid and his wife are around finally as he has stopped running from his responsibilities. They are just hanging out with a newfound appreciation of each other's company and their lot in life.

Neil: (curiously) So are you like cancer free now?

Kris: (matter of fact) Nah, still doing Radiotherapy. It's shit. In comic books they get like superpowers from radiation but all I got is fried nuts. My jizz can literally cause cancer and worst of all, the clinic said no more donations. No more mini me's running around the country. I've pretty much got a nuke in my nut-sack and trust me; you don't want it to fallout.

Kris looks abnormally proud of this average joke until he gets humbled.

Neil: (quip)Like fat man?

Joensy: Nah little boy.

Neil and Jonesy Laugh as Kris looks unimpressed.

Kris: (jokingly) I fucking hate you guys.

All the boys share a smile.

Kris: So, what happened with all the cash we got to make the movie? There was like 25 grand left after we bought that hoverboard and Screen Australia gave ya another 30k. That's like 55k.

Neil: (sarcastically) We spent it on the movie man. Couldn't you tell from the quality?

Kris: No, it looked like you made it in Microsoft Paint.

Neil: Hahaha yeah I did.

Kris: Awesome. But seriously what happened to the cash?

Jonesy: (A bit ashamed) Well, a bit went on the dogs.

Kris: Checks out.

Jonesy: And you two were behind like two years on the rent. No wonder your landlord was always dropping by. Lucky it's my demented Nan that owns this joint, so you didn't get evicted. She had no idea that you blokes never paid but the new us, we're honest, and we do good in the world.

Kris: Amen brother!

Neil: (excitedly) And I used the rest to buy this first edition Charizard!

Kris: *(Bewildered)* Are you serious? So, it's all gone?

Neil: Yeah but look at the card, its shiny as! Proper PSA graded and shit.

Kris examines the card and gives an approving look.

Kris: That is pretty good.

Jonesy: Foods up lads.

Kris: Food? That looks more like cremated remains!!

Rock music plays as the camera zooms out as Jonesy back hands Kris and hands him a plate of food. As the narrator starts to speak.

The scene continues with the boys chilling eating BBQ, playing with Jonesy's kid, having a laugh and a cup of tea. Simply enjoying each other's company and the glory of another compelling day in a life well lived.

The narrator from Kris's nature documentaries (David Attenborough) States the below over this final scene.

David Attenborough: *And so, the boys stand victorious. Not much has changed. To the naked eye, all is as it was in the beginning. Yet their epic journey of triumph and tragedy, mixed with finally taking on some responsibility, has changed their hearts for the better. They are just like you. Friends, family men, regular guys doing their best to look after themselves and each other while facing the challenges of life. They are true Kings of The Backyard.*

THE END

Characters

Leads

Neil
Kris
Jonesy

Medium Speaking Roles

Chinthia
Rollz

Small Speaking Roles

Shop keep
Neils Date
Waiter
Reporter
Clint – Jonesy's Dad
Sheila – Jonesy's mum
Annabelle – Jonesy's wife
Jonesy's baby girl.
Surgeon
Brad the homosexual
Black Guys x 2
Crowd member
Nature Show Narrator – David Attenborough type.

Ensemble

Nurses x 2
Gay man
Cinema Guests

Special Thanks

Thanks to Neil David Ewan for the cover art and illustrations.

To my friends for letting me take the piss out of them without any push back.

To God for giving us the world and the word then allowing me to shape my own world through these words.

To my father who is in heaven. You would've thought this story was hilarious. I can picture you laughing at the shocking jokes in it and winding mum up about what her son has done! Thanks for sharing your humour with me.

To my daughter, all the good that I do in this world is imbued with the love I have for you. You are my motivation. The very air in my lungs that fills me with purpose to go on. Daddies doing everything he can to be with you.

Finally, thank you to everyone who supported me through my battle with cancer and subsequent tragedies. I live today because of you. I don't know if I'm ever going to make it home, if I do, I won't be the same but please know, my love for you will never fade.

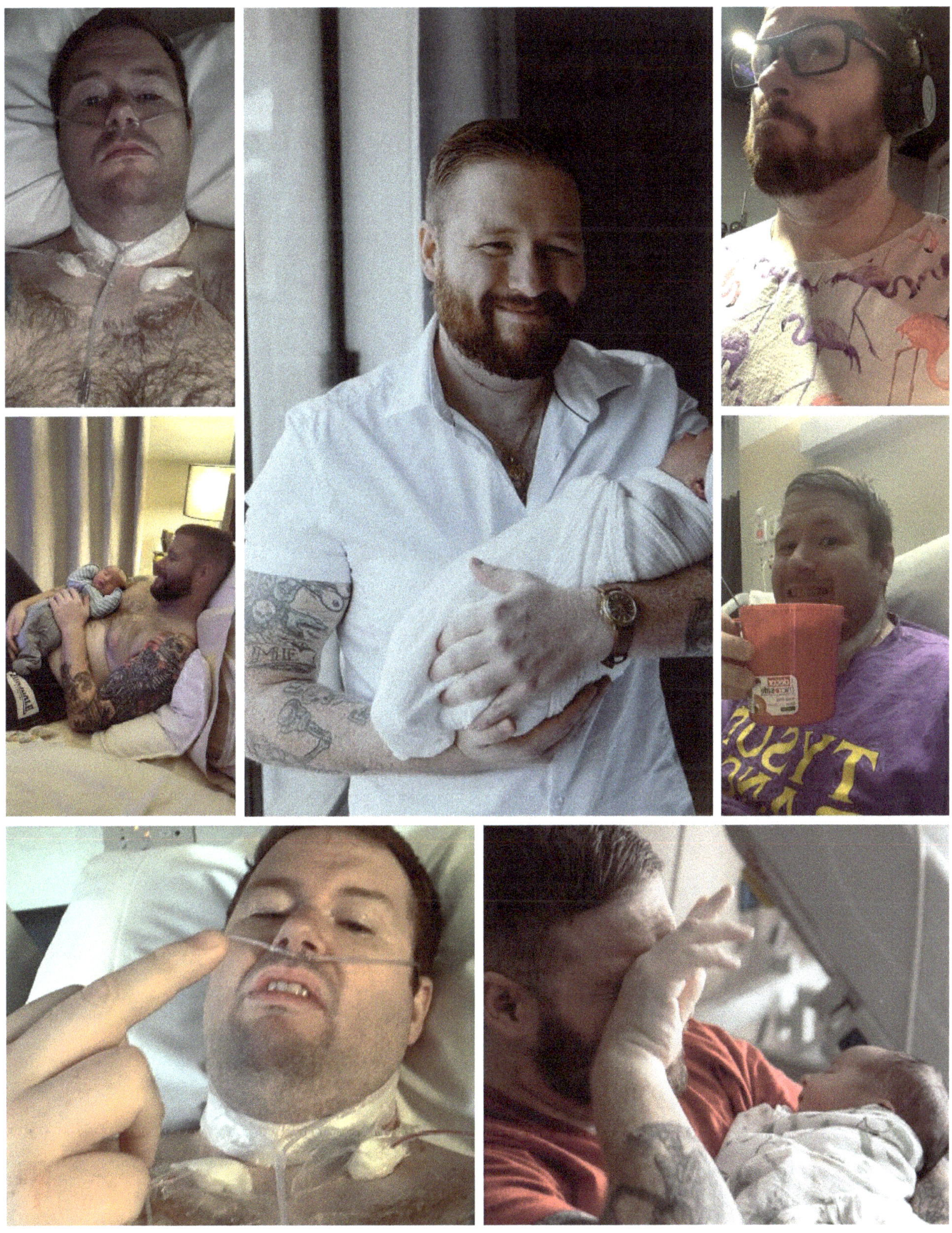

KRISTIAN WILLIAM WRIGHT